AF469633

Also available:
The Birthday Surprise
Winter's Coming
Fun on the Pond

Text © Margaret Carter 1994
Illustrations © Richard Fowler 1994
First published 1994 by
Campbell Books
12 Half Moon Court – London EC1A 7HE

All rights reserved

Printed in Hong Kong

ISBN 1 85292 188 9

Visitors
to Stay

Margaret Carter
Richard Fowler

CAMPBELL BOOKS

Their heads were deep inside their old playbox.

Blackbird brings a message

The Bear family – mother, father and the
three children – Tim, George and Daisy – were
still eating breakfast in their house in the
great Ashridge wood when they heard a tapping
at the window.

'It's Blackbird,' said George, running to
open the window. 'He must have a message
for us.'

Blackbird was the forest's postman.

Now – looking very important – he hopped into the room, 'Grandpa and Grandma Bear send greetings and would like to come for a visit,' he said.

'Hooray,' cried the boys. 'Please tell them they will be most welcome,' said mother. 'Most welcome,' said father. 'Most,' said Daisy who was still learning to talk but didn't like being left out.

Blackbird stayed for a chat and a bowl
of milk but as soon as he'd flown away,
the bears went upstairs to the spare room
at the top of the house, where visitors
always slept when they came to stay.

'It looks rather shabby,' said mother.
'We'll never get it ready in time.'

'Oh we'll all help, won't we, boys?' said
father, but the boys didn't answer. Their
heads were deep inside their old playbox.

'Look at all these things we'd forgotten,'
they called. There was a jigsaw without many
pieces, a ball with a hole in it, books, dolls,
stickers, the head of their old rocking horse . . .

'We'd better get rid of all that,' said
father, 'after all, you never play with them
any more.' But the boys looked so upset
that mother was sorry for them.

'Don't worry,' she said. 'We'll think
of something. I'm sure we can find room for
them somewhere.'

That made them feel better at once.

'Now where's Daisy got to?' she said.
Tim began to giggle. 'Look!' Daisy's face
was looking out from a little cupboard.
She had her baby bonnet on her head and
a tight jumper covering half her tummy.
    'They're your baby clothes,' laughed
mother. 'You've grown out of them now.'
'Mine, mine, mine,' said Daisy clutching
them. Her mouth began to wobble which
meant she might cry. Mother sighed.
'We never seem to get rid of anything,'
she said. 'Oh well, bring them downstairs.'

'Let's make some space so we can paint
the walls,' said father when mother had
gone. 'First we must push all the furniture
into the middle of the room and cover
it with these sheets.'
    'This chair is very heavy,' puffed Tim.
'I can't move it!' There was a little
giggle from beneath the sheet – George
was sitting on the chair. 'Get off
George – no wonder it's too heavy!'
    They both enjoyed stripping off the
old wallpaper. It came away in long
curls (some of which curled round Tim)
but at last it was all finished.
    'I'll dust,' said George. He loved his
feather duster. He whizzed it along the
top of the walls and made so much dust
they all began to sneeze. Then he
tickled Tim's nose which made him sneeze
again. 'Time to stop I think,' said father.

They both enjoyed stripping off the old wallpaper.

By now they were all quite tired. They
sat and looked at the room. 'It will
look better when it's painted,' father
said. 'We'll do that tomorrow.'

'Ooh I love painting,' said George.
'I love the way the brush goes *slap*, *splosh*,
wallop!'

'That's what I'm afraid of,' said father.
'I think *I'll* paint and you can just watch!'
'That won't be much fun,' thought the boys,
'but maybe he'll let us paint just a bit . . .'

Danger! Painters at work!

Father Bear was looking for something
in the small cupboard under the stairs.
The boys could hear him muttering to
himself. 'No . . no . . not that . . .'

'What's he doing?' whispered George.
'Looking for paint for the grandparents'
room,' explained Tim.

At last father stopped muttering and backed
out from the cupboard, a tin of paint in
each paw.

'There's plenty of white paint,' he said.
'So I'll paint it white, but I'll take the blue
paint up as well – just in case.'

They all helped carry the paint and the
brushes upstairs. 'What can we do now?'
asked George. 'You can take that bag of
old wallpaper down,' said father.

The bag was so fat that George could
only just get his arms round it. Only
his ears showed at the top and his feet at
the bottom.

'You look like a walking bag,' laughed Tim.

'I can't see *anything*,' said George –
and then, he tripped. Down the stairs
he slid, sliding, sliding all the way
down as if the bag were a soft sledge.

He landed at the bottom with a bump.

'That was quick,' laughed mother,
picking him up.

George rubbed his head and climbed
upstairs again. 'Shall I paint now?'
he asked. 'No,' said father, '*I'll* paint!'

The boys sat on the bed to watch but
they soon got very bored and began to
push each other off the bed.

'You'd better go downstairs before
you get into mischief,' advised father.
So down they went.

'I've something to show you,' whispered
mother. 'It's a surprise for father.'

'Is it food?' asked Tim. 'No, it
isn't. Come in and you'll see.' And
she shut the door because she didn't
want father to see.

Upstairs on his own, father painted
very quickly. Soon it was all finished.
Now the room was shining white and
clean – but perhaps it looked a little
empty, he thought.

'We're coming upstairs,' called Tim.
'Don't look – we've a surprise for you!'

There was a great deal of bumping
and noise outside the door, then four
brown faces peered round. 'Shut your
eyes,' they called. He did so.

– 'Oh my!' he gasped. 'Oh my!'

A lot more bumping went on.

'Open your eyes Father!' He did as he was told. 'Oh my!' he gasped. 'Oh my!'

On the bed, glowing with the colours of the rainbow, was a patchwork quilt. 'Made from the pieces from Daisy's old dresses,' explained mother. Another quilt covered the old playbox and two dolls without legs had been made into cases for pyjamas.

A mobile swayed in the breeze from the window. 'It's our jig-saw pieces,' said Tim – 'the bits we didn't lose.' Pictures made from old pages hung on the walls but, best of all, was a hanging basket, bright and shining and filled with flowers. 'It's the ball with a hole in it,' George laughed.

'Don't you think we've made good use of all the old toys?' asked mother.

Father could hardly speak for the
surprise. 'It looks wonderful,' he said
at last. 'And *your* painting is wonderful
as well,' they said. And if bears could
blush then father would have blushed.

'We've all worked really hard,' he
said. 'I think we should go down now
and have a rest.' But they were all
so busy talking about grandpa and
grandma's visit that they didn't notice
one thing. Daisy was missing!

Daisy in trouble!

'Now, where has Daisy got to?' said mother.
They had all been so busy talking about what
they would do when the grandparents came to
stay that they hadn't noticed Daisy wasn't
with them.

'I expect she's upstairs,' said Tim.
'I'll go and get her,' and he ran out of the
room calling, 'Daisy! Daisy!'

Suddenly there was a terrible shriek!
'Aah!' it sounded. Then there was another
sound – very quick feet running downstairs.
Father jumped up so quickly that his chair
fell over. 'What's the matter?' he cried.
'Whatever's happening?'

'It's Tim playing a trick,' said George
and he went to look . . but then there was
another loud shriek – 'Aah!' – and this time
it was George. Quickly father and mother
ran to the doorway . . . 'Look, look!' Tim said.
He pointed with a shaking paw.

Standing at the top of the stairs was
a very small white ghost!

'Look at his terrible eyes,' cried Tim.
'Look at his terrible face,' stammered his
brother. The ghost took a step towards them.
   They all fell back. George fell on Tim;
Tim fell on mother; mother fell on father.
Father didn't fall on anyone as there was no
one to fall on to. He stayed upright.

   'Look!' Mother was pointing to the floor
where little white footsteps led from the
bedroom to the ghost. 'Ghosts don't have
footsteps,' she said. 'They *glide*! It can't
be a ghost,' and she began to smile.

Then something very sad happened. Two big tears plopped out of the ghost's eyes and ran slowly down its cheeks. Where the tears ran they left behind two brown streaks.

'It's Daisy!' said George. 'She's been playing with the paint!' The lids were off the tins of white paint. 'Oh, look at the wall!' whispered Tim.

On the clean white wall were several blue blobs, paw-sized blobs.

The tears were running very quickly down
the cheeks of the little white ghost. 'She
didn't mean it, father,' said George. The
boys hated to see Daisy cry although she was
a terrible nuisance sometimes.

'Not mean,' said Daisy and hiccoughed.

'I know you didn't, Daisy,' said father. 'We shouldn't have left you upstairs on your own.' 'I know what to do!' said Tim, who had been looking at the wall, and he said something very quietly to George.

'Yes!' shouted George. Both began to search in the old playbox, flinging out all their broken toys – a skipping rope, the head of their old rocking horse. 'Here it is,' said Tim and he pulled out a piece of cardboard. Carefully he unfolded it to show a long picture of fields with cows and horses, roads and little houses.

Then far away they saw the grandparents coming –

'It's our old frizz,' said George. '*Frieze*,' said Tim, 'but if we stuck it along the bottom of the wall and waggled the blue blobs about to look like clouds . . .' he stopped.

'It would look lovely,' said mother, 'and no one would know what had happened!'

'Hooray!' cried the boys and even father smiled. Daisy stopped crying and sniffed. She opened her mouth to smile but some paint ran into it so she closed it again.

'It's a bath for you, my girl,' said mother.
So while mother took Daisy to the bathroom
the boys helped father to stick the frieze
along the bottom of the wall. Then they
painted wiggly edges round the blobs so they
looked like blue clouds on a white wall.

They stepped back to look. The effect
was charming.

'Tweet, tweet, that looks sweet,' sang a voice.
It was Blackbird on the windowsill. 'You're
just in time,' he said. 'I passed your visitors
on the way here.'

At once there was great activity. Paint put
away, a dust with the feather duster – all was
ready. They sighed with happiness.

Then far away they saw the grandparents
coming and they all ran to meet them. What hugs
and kisses there were, what excitement.

They all climbed the stairs together – it was
rather a squash but they managed. 'This is the
nicest room I've ever seen,' said grandma.
'It's quite lovely!'

No one told the grandparents what had
happened although Daisy hid her face in mother's
apron. 'Hello, what's this?' asked grandpa,
picking up something from the floor.

'It's the head of our old rocking horse,'
said Tim sadly. 'We did love it so but now it
won't stick on anymore. It's no use now.'

'I don't know about that,' said grandpa.
'We might think of something.'

He looked at them with his kind eyes and
the boys knew at once that grandpa would
be able to help. 'It's going to be a lovely
time,' said Tim. 'We're so glad you've
come to stay with us,' said George.